The LAST FIREHAWK

The Underland

by
Katrina Charman

BRANCHES

SCHOLASTIC INC.

The LAST FIREHAWK

Read All the Books

1 The Last Firehawk: The Ember Stone

2 The Last Firehawk: The Crystal Caverns

3 The Last Firehawk: The Whispering Oak

4 The Last Firehawk: Lullaby Lake

5 The Last Firehawk: The Shadowlands

6 The Last Firehawk: The Battle for Perodia

7 The Last Firehawk: The Cloud Kingdom

8 The Last Firehawk: The Silver Swamp

9 The Last Firehawk: The Golden Temple

10 The Last Firehawk: The Secret Maze

11 The Last Firehawk: The Underland

12 The Last Firehawk: The Shadow Returns

scholastic.com/lastfirehawk

Table of Contents

For Brick, Piper, and Riley. –KC

Library of Congress Cataloging-in-Publication Data

Names: Charman, Katrina, author. | Tondora, Judit, illustrator. | Charman, Katrina. Last firehawk ; 11. Title: The Underland / Katrina Charman ; [Illustrated by Judit Tondora] Description: First edition. | New York : Branches/Scholastic Inc., 2022. | Series: The last firehawk ; 11 | Audience: Ages 6–8. | Audience: Grades 2–3. | Summary: Tag and Skyla have returned to Perodia to begin their warrior training, but when their friend Blaze returns with troubling news that her mother has gone missing, Tag and Skyla's warrior skills are quickly put to the test.
Identifiers: LCCN 2021059269 | ISBN 9781338832525 (paperback) | ISBN 9781338832532 (library binding)
Subjects: LCSH: Owls—Juvenile fiction. | Squirrels—Juvenile fiction. | Animals, Mythical—Juvenile fiction. | Magic—Juvenile fiction. | Good and evil—Juvenile fiction. | Adventure stories. | CYAC: Owls—Fiction. | Squirrels—Fiction. | Animals, Mythical—Fiction. | Magic—Fiction. | Good and evil—Fiction. | Adventure and adventurers—Fiction. | Fantasy. | LCGFT: Action and adventure fiction.
Classification: LCC PZ7.1.C495 Un 2022 | DDC [Fic] —dc23
LC record available at https://lccn.loc.gov/2021059269

10 9 8 7 6 5 4 3 2 1   22 23 24 25 26

Printed in China   62

First edition, November 2022
Illustrated by Judit Tondora
Edited by Rachel Matson
Book design by Jaime Lucero

∼ INTRODUCTION∼

Tag, a small barn owl, and his friend
Skyla, a squirrel, have returned home to Valor Wood.
Six weeks have passed since their return from the Land
of the Firehawks. Tag and Skyla were made Owls of
Valor after they helped to destroy The Shadow and
save the Land of Perodia. Now, they are training to
be warriors with Maximus, the captain of the Owls
of Valor.

Tag and Skyla's friend Blaze has returned to the
Land of the Firehawks with her mother, the leader
of the firehawks. The friends can visit each other
anytime because of a permanent portal between the
two lands.

Claw, who was once the evil vulture Thorn, is now
good. He has become friends with Tag, Skyla, and
Blaze. And he has been using his magic to fix all the
bad things he did with The Shadow.

But strange things have been happening across
Perodia. The friends will need to reunite and work
together before a powerful enemy returns.

The adventure continues . . .

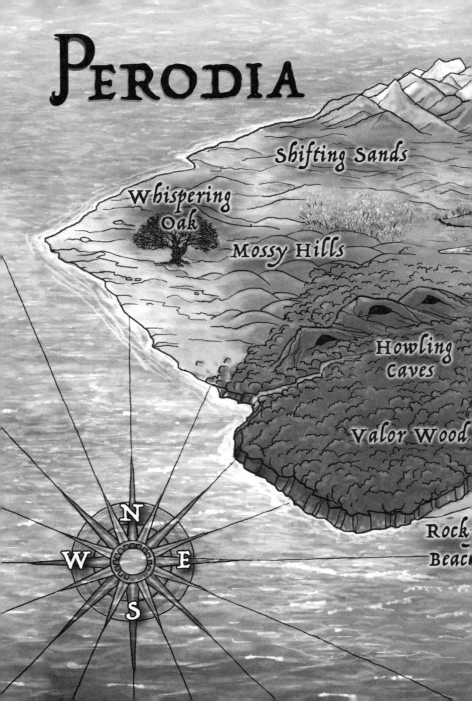

Crystal Caverns
Jagged Mountains
Bubbling Bog
Lullaby Lake
The Shadowlands
Blue Bay
Fire Island

TRAINING TIME

TA-RAA TA-RA TA-RA!

Tag jumped out of his nest as the horns trumpeted around the forest. He grabbed his dagger and pulled on his armor.

It was time for training!

"Skyla!" Tag called up to the top branches of the tree, where his best friend lived.

But Skyla was already ready to go. She leaped from branch to branch, and Tag flew after her. They landed at a big tree stump in a clearing of the wood.

More Owls of Valor in training flew down to join them. Everyone waited for Maximus. Tag and Skyla had been training for six weeks now: learning how to fight, how to sneak up on enemies, and how to use the forest's magic.

Tag couldn't wait to be sent on a mission. But every time he asked Maximus or Grey, the leader of the Owls of Valor, they said he wasn't ready.

A row of wooden swords lay on the ground. Tag looked at them, feeling worried. He was good with his dagger. But the swords were long and heavy, and his wings were smaller than everyone else's.

Maximus flew in. "Choose a weapon!" he ordered.

Skyla grinned at Tag. She chose the longest sword. It was taller than she was!

Tag waited as the other owls chose their weapons. Then he stepped forward.

He groaned. All that was left was an old, chipped sword. He lifted it with his wing. Luckily, it wasn't too heavy.

"Choose a partner!" Maximus yelled. "Swing and jab! Swing and jab!" Maximus attacked a nearby tree to demonstrate.

Tag looked to Skyla, but another owl had already chosen her for a partner. Tag turned to see the only young owl left.

Bod.

Bod was twice as big as Tag and a bully.

Tag tried not to let Bod see his wings shake as he lifted his sword.

Bod grinned, then
swung his sword fast.
He knocked Tag's sword
from his wings before
Tag had a chance to
move!

"Hey!" Tag grumbled.
"I wasn't ready yet."

He bent to lift up his
sword. Bod stepped forward, jabbing Tag
in the back and knocking him over.

"Never turn your back on your enemy,
Tag!" Maximus shouted.

Tag narrowed his eyes as Bod smirked.

"Tag! Skyla!" Maximus called.

Skyla landed beside Tag. They saluted
their leader.

"I have some news," Maximus told them.
"It's time for you to go out on your first
mission."

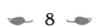

THE MISSION

Tag bounced happily. "Our first mission for the Owls of Valor!" he said.

"Where are we going?" Skyla asked. Her tail curled excitedly.

"Fire Island?" Tag said. "Or maybe the Howling Caves?"

"What about the Crystal Caverns?" asked Skyla. "Are the ice leopards causing trouble?"

Maximus shook his head.

"There have been some strange reports," he said. "You are to go on patrol at the edge of Valor Wood with Bod and look out for anything unusual."

Bod stood beside Maximus and gave Tag a small smile.

Tag frowned. "We don't need Bod to come with us," he moaned.

Skyla crossed her arms and nodded. She didn't like Bod, ever since he'd stepped on her tail the first day of training.

"Bod has been training for longer than you two," Maximus said.

"But we've been on dangerous missions," Skyla protested. "We found all the pieces of the Ember Stone!"

"And we found the Land of the Firehawks," Tag said.

"And we stopped The Shadow!" Skyla added.

Bod stared at Skyla. "I thought your friend *Blaze* did all that?" he said. "You couldn't have done any of it without a firehawk."

Skyla growled and took a step forward, but Tag held her back.

"That's enough!" Maximus said. "You are going on this mission together. Teamwork is an important part of being an Owl of Valor."

He flew off.

Bod sneered at Skyla. "Maybe you should stay here?" he said. "After all, you're not really an *Owl* of Valor, are you? You're just a squirrel."

Skyla scowled at Bod and stomped away.

Tag went after her. *I wonder what strange things have been happening in the wood,* he thought. *Maybe this mission will lead to our next big adventure?*

ON PATROL

Tag, Skyla, and Bod began their mission as the sun set behind the trees.

Tag and Bod flew through the purple-orange sky. Skyla jumped from branch to branch below.

They were headed for a part of Valor Wood that Tag had never been to. The ground was covered with soft green moss and small piles of soil. It looked like burrows or holes had been dug there.

Skyla jumped to the ground and peered inside one of the big holes. "It goes a long way down," she said, her voice echoing. She dropped an acorn into the hole. But there was no sound of it hitting the bottom.

Tag and Bod landed beside her.

"Hmm," Tag said. "I wonder who made these holes?"

Bod gave a big yawn. "Probably just moles or mice or something," he said. "This is so boring!"

"Then why don't *you* go home and leave the patrolling to us," Skyla snapped.

Bod rolled his eyes.

They walked on through the woods, looking for anything strange or unusual.

Bod wandered off into the trees. But then he froze. "Did you see that?" he whispered.

Tag peered in Bod's direction. "I don't see anything," he said.

The leaves rustled. Then suddenly —

WHOOSH! Something small, gray, and very fast raced past them, almost knocking Tag over.

Bod screamed and flew in the opposite direction.

"Bod!" Tag called. "We have to stay together."

But Bod was gone.

Tag pulled out his dagger and Skyla reached for her slingshot. They chased after the small gray creature.

"It's so fast!" Skyla called from the trees.

"It is *too* fast for a normal animal!" Tag puffed.

Skyla flipped out of the tree and landed on the creature's back. It fell into the dirt facedown.

"Gotcha!" she shouted.

Tag landed beside her, holding his dagger tight. Then he frowned. Skyla had just trapped a mole! It was smaller than Tag, with light gray fur and a small, twitchy tail.

"We are Owls of Valor," Skyla said. "Did something scare you? Do you need our help?"

The mole turned slowly to face them.

Tag and Skyla gasped and jumped back.

It was no ordinary mole. It had orange eyes!

THE DISCOVERY

"**T**ag!" Skyla cried, gripping her slingshot. "The mole has orange eyes, just like Thorn's spies!"

Tag took a step toward the mole. "We don't want to hurt you," he said. "What happened to you?"

19

But before Tag could move any closer, the mole quickly dug a new hole. Then it disappeared into it.

Skyla's voice shook. "The last time we saw orange eyes was when Thorn turned normal animals into his army of spies."

"But Thorn is Claw now," Tag said. "And Claw is good."

"I know that *was* true . . ." Skyla replied. "But what if The Shadow has returned and made him bad again?" She glanced around. "Where did Bod go?"

Tag shook his head. "He ran away! What a scaredy-owl."

The sound of footsteps came up behind them. They were loud and heavy. And they were getting closer.

Skyla grabbed Tag's wing. "What if there are more moles with orange eyes?" she said. "There could be a whole army!"

Before they could hide, a large creature burst through the trees. Tag and Skyla gasped, and their eyes went as wide as the full moon!

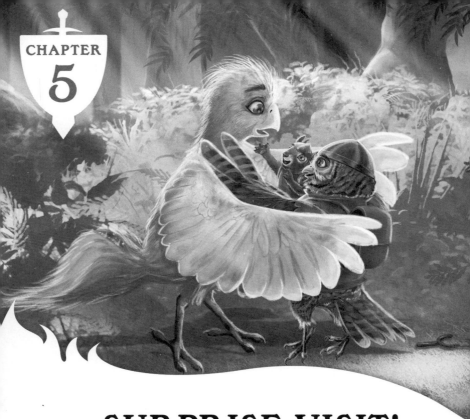

SURPRISE VISIT!

Skyla dropped her slingshot. "Blaze!" she cried.

The firehawk gave her friends a hug, pulling them into her orange-and-red wings.

Blaze's eyes filled with shiny tears. "I need your help!" she said. "My mom has gone missing. I think something terrible has happened to her."

"Oh no!" Tag said, patting Blaze's wing. "What has happened to Talia?"

Blaze sniffled. "My mom went through a portal to another land. She said she would only be gone for a few days. But she never came back, and then we got a fire message."

"What's a fire message?" Skyla asked.

"It's something that firehawks can do," Blaze said. "I have learned how to do it, too. You can send a message or an object to other firehawks through fire. I'll show you."

Blaze waved her wing in the air. Her feathers lit up with small flames. She drew a picture of Tag and Skyla in the air. It burned in front of them for a while, then turned into black wisps of smoke and disappeared.

"That's a fire message," Blaze said. "I've let the firehawks know that I have found you."

"What was Talia's message?" Tag asked.

Blaze pulled out a long silver feather. "She sent one of her magical tail feathers. I think she needs our help."

"Did her message say anything?" Skyla asked.

CRACK!

There was a loud noise behind them. Tag drew his dagger. "Who's there?" he called.

Bod crept out from the trees.

Skyla put her paws on her hips and glared at him. "You ran away!" she cried. "Owls of Valor are supposed to stick together."

Bod stared at the ground. "When I saw the mole's orange eyes, I got scared. I thought The Shadow was back."

Blaze's eyes flared. "The Shadow?" she said.

"Just before you arrived, we saw a mole with orange eyes. And it was fast, too fast for a normal mole," Tag told Blaze.

Skyla sighed. "I think we had better talk to the creature who knows the most about The Shadow. Let's go and find Claw."

THE SHADOWLANDS

The friends and Bod headed for Claw's home in the Shadowlands as the sun rose. Skyla rode on Blaze's back, while Tag and Bod followed.

Back when Claw had been Thorn, the Shadowlands were dark and dry. Everything was brown and the plants were dying.

But now, Claw used his magic for good. Flowers in rainbow colors covered the ground. Beautiful plants and trees bloomed. And many animals and insects had returned to the land. Tag could see colorful butterflies and bees floating over the flowers.

Our friend Claw can't *have had anything to do with the mole or Talia's disappearance*, Tag thought. He was sure of it.

They landed in a small clearing. The smell of the flowers was so wonderful that Skyla took in a deep breath and sighed happily.

Claw was sitting on a large rock, watering some flowers. He noticed his friends and flew over to them with a big smile. Then he saw Blaze's sad face.

"What's wrong?" Claw asked Blaze.

"Talia has gone missing," Tag told Claw.

"We think that The Shadow might have something to do with it," Skyla added.

Claw shook his head. "Blaze destroyed The Shadow," he said.

"But we saw a mole with orange eyes!" Bod blurted out. He was hiding behind Blaze.

Claw narrowed his eyes. "Who are you?" he asked.

"That's Bod," Tag said. "He's training as an Owl of Valor."

"When he's not running away to hide," Skyla mumbled.

Bod's face turned red and he glared at Skyla.

Claw frowned as he turned back to Tag. "The mole had orange eyes?" he asked.

"And it was super-fast, like it had magical powers," Tag said.

Claw looked at his friends. "We need to speak with Grey at once. Perodia could be in great danger."

They took to the sky with Bod following and quickly arrived back in Valor Wood.

They found Grey near the giant tree stump. When the leader of the Owls of Valor saw them, he hurried over.

Blaze told Grey about Talia, and Tag told him about the mole with orange eyes.

"I was afraid of this," Grey said. "Maximus heard that animals throughout the forest have been reported missing. I fear Perodia may be in great danger."

CHAPTER 7

AN ENEMY RETURNS

Bod and the friends followed Grey up into his tree. They walked up the spiral staircase to the very top, where Grey kept his books.

Grey searched his books frantically. Then he found one and shouted loudly.

"Aha! It's right here!" he said. "How could I have missed this?"

"What is it?" Claw asked.

They gathered closer to read the book.

"The Shadow is an ancient magic," Grey read. "Older than even the first firehawk's egg. It finds other power-hungry creatures to use its dark magic. As long as the magic exists, so does The Shadow."

"But Blaze defeated The Shadow with the Ember Stone!" Skyla cried.

Grey nodded. "I thought so. But now I think that was only a *piece* of The Shadow that we defeated. Perhaps another piece lived on and found a new evil creature."

"And now it has grown more powerful!" Tag said. His head felt dizzy at the thought of The Shadow returning.

"The Shadow must have found someone like Thorn who wanted to use its dark magic for evil. The missing animals and the orange-eyed creature you saw could mean that The Shadow is working with someone new and creating an army again," Grey said.

Blaze's feathers shook. "They must have taken my mom!"

"But where?" Tag asked. "Can you check your maps, Grey?"

Grey pulled out some papers from a pile and blew the dust off.

"I do have one special map," he said. "It shows you things that are lost. Maybe it can show us where Talia is."

He waved his wing over the map. Pink and purple lights sparkled across the paper, but it stayed blank.

Grey frowned. "Hmm. That should have worked," he said.

He lifted the map to take a closer look.

"What's that?" Bod asked, pointing to the underside of the map.

Grey turned it over. A tiny dot glowed pink.

"But there's nothing on that side," he said. "Unless . . ."

Grey's face went pale. He quickly grabbed another book and flicked through it.

"I have heard of a hidden land," Grey said slowly. "But I thought it was only a myth. I didn't think it could be real."

"What is it?" Blaze asked.

"The Underland," Grey said shakily. "It is a dark and dangerous place, hidden deep beneath the surface of Perodia. If Talia is trapped there, she is in very great danger."

THE PORTAL

Grey looked at Tag, Skyla, Blaze, Bod, and Claw. His eyes crinkled with worry.

"Whatever is happening, it must be coming from the Underland," Grey said. "I am sending you on a new mission. Blaze will create a portal to the Underland. You must find Talia and discover who The Shadow is working with."

Tag took a deep breath. *This is my scariest mission so far*, he thought. *But I have to help Blaze's mom and stop The Shadow.*

"The Underland is a bad place. If The Shadow is there, you will be surrounded by enemies," Grey warned.

He opened a wide wooden chest carved with images of the Owls of Valor. Then he pulled out a glass globe hanging on a twisted wire. A light inside the globe glowed green.

"This is a magical lantern," Grey told them. "There is no light at all in the Underland: no sun, no moon, no stars. The lantern will help guide your way. It will always stay lit."

Skyla's eyes glowed as she took the lantern. "Wow!"

Grey reached into the chest again and pulled out something else. He handed it to Bod. It was

a long sword made of shiny silver with an engraved wooden handle.

Bod stared at the
sword, his eyes wide
and gleaming.

"You will need a
weapon when you go
into the Underland,"
Grey told Bod.

Tag groaned.
"We don't need
Bod's help!"

Grey put a
wing on Tag's
shoulder. "I
remember when
I sent another
young owl and squirrel
on an important mission," he said. He
looked at Tag and Skyla. "They proved
themselves to be brave warriors. I think
Bod deserves a chance, too."

Tag looked at the ground. Grey was right. He should give Bod a chance.

"Are you ready, Blaze?" Tag asked.

Blaze nodded. "This is a powerful magical object," she said, holding Talia's magical tail feather. The feather began to glow, brighter and brighter, but the room around them grew dark. A swirling hole appeared in the floor. It was silvery black.

"Good luck!" Claw called out as Skyla, Blaze, and Bod jumped into the portal one by one.

Tag stepped forward and waited to fall. But instead, his foot landed on a cold, damp step. He looked back — Grey and Claw had disappeared. All he could see was the swirling light of the portal. He took another step forward, into the darkness.

THE UNDERLAND

Tag walked down the stairs. He shivered. The air around him was damp and cold. Up ahead he could see the green glow of Grey's magical lantern. He followed the light until he found his friends and took the last step.

44

The new ground beneath his feet was wet and sticky. It felt like mud mixed with tiny stones.

"Let's find Talia and get out of here," Skyla said with a shudder.

The glow from the lantern was bright, but it was hard to see much around them. Blaze ruffled her feathers and they lit up, helping to light the way.

Tag was thankful for Blaze's magic. The flames from her wings were bright and warm, and he stayed close to her as they walked.

All around them, tree roots reached out of the ground, as if the trees were planted upside down. The roots looked like twisty, spiky claws trying to grab them.

Strings of dead moss hung from the roots and dripped with oozing black liquid.

Tag shuddered. It reminded him of how the Shadowlands used to be. But the Underland was colder, darker, and much scarier.

It's too quiet here, Tag thought. There didn't seem to be any signs of life. No birds, no animals, no bugs.

Skyla moved closer to Tag on one side. Bod moved so close to him on the other side that they bumped wings. Tag could feel Bod's feathers shaking and hear his beak chattering.

"It's okay to be scared," Tag told Bod. "I'm scared, too."

Bod gave Tag a small smile. "I'm glad Blaze is with us," he said. "She is amazing."

Tag smiled. "She is," he said.

"You and Skyla are, too," Bod admitted. "You saved Perodia when you defeated The Shadow."

"We did it together, as a team," Tag said. "That's what being an Owl of Valor is all about."

Suddenly, Blaze stopped walking. "I think we've been this way already," she said.

Skyla groaned. "How can you tell? Everything looks the same here!"

Tag sighed. How were they ever going to find Talia?

"We should take a break," he told them.

Just then there was a loud **POP!** A light soared overhead, brightening the darkness. It hovered above them like a guiding star.

"Did you see that fireball?!" Blaze cried, jumping up. "It's one of my mom's. She is showing us the way!"

CHAPTER 10

TALIA'S WARNING

Blaze raced off in the direction of the fireball.

"Blaze, wait!" Skyla called. But Blaze ignored her and hurried on.

Skyla turned to Tag. "How does Blaze know that light came from Talia?" she asked. "How would Talia know we are here?"

"It could be a trap," Bod warned.

Tag scratched his head. "Something doesn't feel right," he agreed. "But we have no other clues."

They chased after Blaze, following her brightly glowing feathers. Slowly, the twisty tree roots disappeared, and they found Blaze waiting up ahead.

"Look!" Blaze called out.

She was pointing to a massive rock. It reached up to the sky and stretched out in both directions. In the center was a perfectly round hole.

"It looks like someone dug into the rock," Bod said.

"Something like the mole with the orange eyes?" Skyla asked. "Moles are good diggers."

"Or something much, much bigger," Tag said.

Bod backed away. "I don't think going in there is a good idea," he said. "I think we should go back to Perodia."

Blaze shook her head. "I have to find my mom!" she said.

"You don't have to come inside if you don't want to," Tag said kindly. "You can keep guard out here."

Skyla held out the lantern to Bod.

Bod took the lantern and nodded. He gripped his sword tightly in his other wing.

Blaze raised her wings and created a fireball, ready to attack. Skyla loaded her slingshot with an acorn, and Tag held out his dagger. The three friends looked at each other, took a deep breath, and then stepped into the opening.

They walked through a long tunnel that went down and down. Tag watched their shadows dance on the walls as they moved. He was glad that Blaze could light the way.

Suddenly, a cold breeze ruffled his feathers. Blaze's feathers flickered and her flames went out.

"Blaze?" Tag called.

Skyla moved closer to Blaze and Tag.

"My magic won't work anymore!" Blaze replied.

Then in the darkness, two blinking orange lights appeared. Then more.

Tag looked closer. He realized that they weren't lights at all.

Glowing orange eyes stared back at them. They were surrounded.

THE RAT KING

Tag, Skyla, and Blaze huddled together in the dark tunnel.

The orange-eyed creatures stared at them. There were all kinds of underground animals: moles, badgers, even a few fluffy bunnies. They seemed to be under a spell, just like Thorn's spies had been.

"We can help you!" Skyla cried as the spies moved closer.

She looked at Tag.

"Blaze, use your magic," Tag whispered. Skyla nodded. "Try your firehawk cry!"

Blaze opened her beak, but no sound came out. She frowned. "My magic isn't working!" she said.

Two large badgers stepped forward. They grabbed the friends and pushed them down the path.

"Where are you taking us?" Skyla demanded. She tried to wriggle away from the badger, but he was impossibly strong.

Tag saw a dull glow at the end of the tunnel. They found themselves standing inside a wide open cavern. Fire torches stuck out of the walls. Their light shone dimly.

In the center of the cavern was the biggest rat Tag had ever seen.

Tag gulped. The rat was white with red eyes and a long, thick tail that trailed down to the ground. He sat on a throne made from the same twisted roots they had seen outside. Long, sharp thorns stuck out from the roots. And on his head, the rat wore a crown made from bones!

Beside the rat sat a twisted wooden cage. There was a shadowy figure inside. *Is that The Shadow?* Tag thought. But then the figure moved into the light.

"Mom!" Blaze cried.

A dark cloud swirled around Talia. She saw Blaze and her eyes went wide. Then she pointed her beak toward three empty cages next to her.

Is she telling us to run? Tag wondered.

"What have you done to her?" Blaze shouted at the huge rat.

The rat smiled. "Let's welcome our guests!" he snarled.

There was a loud rumble and the room filled with rats. They ran along the ground like a river of brown and white and gray. They lifted the friends and threw Tag and Skyla into two of the empty cages.

Blaze tried to fight the rats off, but they tied up her beak with thick black vines. Finally, they put her into the third cage.

Then the dark cloud that surrounded Talia split in two. One half stayed with her, and the other floated over to Blaze.

The rat laughed as Blaze struggled to use her magic.

"It's no use," the rat laughed again. "The Shadow has bound your magic. It won't work here."

Tag's heart dropped. Blaze had no magic, and they were trapped!

TRAPPED!

The rat loomed over them. He paced back and forth in front of their cages and grinned a wide grin that showed off his long, yellow teeth.

"Who are you?" Tag asked.

"Why did you take Blaze's mom?" Skyla added.

The rat smiled. "I am Skull. King of the rats!" he said. "I needed the firehawk to open a portal so we could travel to Perodia," he continued. "But she refused. So instead, we trapped her here. We knew the firehawks would send someone after her."

Skull leaned in close to Tag. His eyes were completely red and his rotten teeth were covered in black slime.

"My spies waited until you arrived in the Underland. They hid in the darkness and used some of The Shadow's magic to keep the portal from closing. Now we can use *your* portal. *And* we have the famous firehawk Blaze and her friends out of the way. You won't be able to defeat The Shadow this time!" Skull said.

Tag held his breath as Skull spoke. The rat smelled like rotting leaves and dead things.

"I was born here in the Underland," Skull told them. "Here we have no light, only darkness. And where there is no light, only dark things grow. We live off scraps and dirt."

Skull looked over at the dark cloud that swirled around Blaze and Talia.

"Then The Shadow came to me!" Skull continued. "It offered me a powerful, dark magic. It whispered to me in my dreams. It told me that I could live in a land above, where I would have everything I wanted and be king of Perodia!"

"The Shadow doesn't care about you!" Tag shouted. "It only wants to use you to gain more power for itself."

Skyla nodded. "It did the same thing to our friend Claw. We are Owls of Valor. We can help you and the other creatures who live here. You don't have to use The Shadow's magic."

Skull shook his head. "You can't give me power!" he snarled. "My army is ready. And now there is nothing standing in our way."

He turned to his army. "To the portal!" Skull commanded.

All around him, his army cheered and yelled. They raised their weapons in the air. Then they started running out of the tunnel.

"You can't leave us here!" Skyla yelled.

Skull laughed, and the sound boomed around the room.

"I *can*!" he said. "Now you will see what it's like to live in the Underland!"

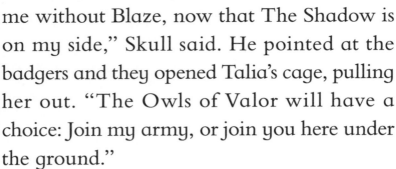

"The Owls of Valor will stop you!" Tag said.

"They can't stop me without Blaze, now that The Shadow is on my side," Skull said. He pointed at the badgers and they opened Talia's cage, pulling her out. "The Owls of Valor will have a choice: Join my army, or join you here under the ground."

Talia shook her head at Skull.

The dark cloud grew bigger around her until Tag couldn't see her anymore.

Blaze banged at her wooden cage while Skyla yelled.

When The Shadow cleared, Talia stood still. She stared at Blaze, but she didn't move or blink. Her eyes were now as orange as her feathers.

"The leader of the firehawks is on my side now, too. Enjoy your new home!" Skull said.

Talia and the army followed Skull out of the tunnel. Blaze banged on the wooden cage again and again. But Talia never looked back.

THE CAGE

Tag sat on the floor of the cage and put his head in his wings. "We fell right into The Shadow's trap! Now Skull is bringing The Shadow back to Perodia!"

The sound of the army marching toward the portal echoed through the tunnel.

Blaze gave a muffled peep from her cage.

"It's not your fault, Blaze," Tag told her. "We just need to find a way out of here and stop Skull. At least I still have my dagger!"

He pulled it out and cut at the vines around his cage, and Skyla used her sharp teeth to chew them. But the vines were too strong.

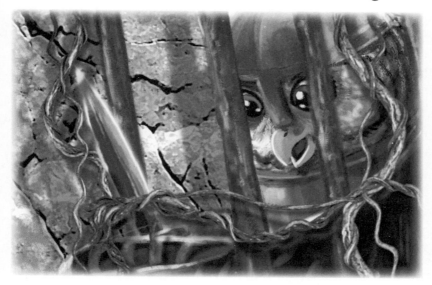

"It's no good!" Skyla sighed. "We're stuck if Blaze can't use her magic. Skull will be at the portal soon!"

Tag thought about Bod standing guard outside the tunnel. *Has Bod been captured, too?* he wondered.

A small, shiny tear rolled down Blaze's face. It dripped off the end of her beak.

"Don't cry!" a voice whispered.

Tag glanced around. At the end of the tunnel, a dim green light swung back and forth, moving closer. "Who's there?" Tag called.

"It's me, Bod!" the voice replied. "I've come to rescue you."

Tag sighed in relief.

Bod emerged from the darkness, holding the lantern.

"I've never been so happy to see you!" Skyla called out.

Bod inspected the cages.

"The cages are strong," he said. "But not as strong as me."

He went to Tag's cage first. He gripped a twisty branch with each wing. Then he pulled as hard as he could.

There was a loud **CRACK** and the wood broke! Tag squeezed out of the cage. Then Bod went to free Skyla and Blaze. He used his sword to cut away the vines around Blaze's beak.

"Let's stop that rat and get my mom back!" Blaze shouted. She flapped her wings, and they blazed with flames, brighter than Tag had ever seen them. The swirling dark cloud around her faded to gold, then disappeared. Then she flew down the tunnel like a fireball, racing toward the portal.

THE RAT ARMY

The friends flew through the Underland. Bod led the way with the lantern.

"Thanks for coming back for us," Tag said.

Bod smiled. "That's what being an Owl of Valor is all about," he said.

Tag scanned the ground ahead. When he saw the army, he hooted and they landed.

"The army has almost reached the portal," Tag told his friends.

Blaze's flames flared. "We have to stop them!"

But before Tag could make a plan, Blaze quickly flew off. Bod and Tag flew after her, and Skyla leaped through the twisted tree roots. Finally, they reached the swirling gray portal.

"Oh no!" Bod said, his wings trembling. "We're too late!"

Skull stood in front of the portal, preparing his army to enter Perodia. The Shadow loomed high above him. It crackled with thunder and lightning and grew bigger and bigger, making the Underland seem even darker.

SKRAAA! Blaze let out her powerful firehawk cry.

The army held their paws over their ears and looked to the sky in horror. Some of them ran away.

Blaze sent out flaming fireballs. She shot at the trees, setting them on fire to light the darkness.

Tag gasped. Now that it was easier to see, he realized just how big the army was.

"Perodia will be destroyed if they get through the portal!" Skyla cried.

She loaded her slingshot and started hitting the army with acorns and stones.

"We need to block the portal," Tag told Bod.

Bod nodded, and they fought their way to the portal entrance.

Just as they were getting close, a bright light appeared within the portal. It was almost blinding! Blurry shapes moved inside the portal, getting closer.

CHAPTER 15

THE BATTLE

Suddenly, Grey flew out of the portal! **SHRIEK!**

Behind him flew Maximus and the Owls of Valor and Claw! One by one, they flew out of the portal and soared overhead. Tag and Bod hugged each other in relief.

Help had arrived!

"Owls of Valor! Attack!" Maximus yelled.

The Owls of Valor swooped down and
chased the army from the portal.

Claw and Grey flew around The Shadow.
They blasted it with their magic. But The
Shadow fought back. Every time Claw shot a
blast of magic at The Shadow, it sent out a dark
cloud in return. Flashes of lightning and crashes
of thunder erupted inside the dark cloud.

On the ground, Tag, Skyla, Bod, and Blaze fought any creature who tried to come near the portal.

As Grey and Claw continued to blast The Shadow, some of the orange-eyed creatures broke free from its spell. Skyla led the animals to the portal so that they could return to Perodia.

Maximus landed behind Tag, breathing heavily. "The Shadow is too strong," he said. "And there are too many enemies. We need to leave!"

Tag, Bod, and Skyla moved closer to the portal and prepared to jump through.

"Blaze, can you close the portal?" Tag asked.

"I can't leave my mom behind!" Blaze cried.

"I'll get her," Bod told Blaze. He flew off.

Bod bravely held out his sword. He battled the two badgers who were holding Talia.

Blaze sent a fireball at The Shadow. It exploded and Talia broke free from the spell, her eyes back to normal. She flew over to Blaze.

"We need to close the portal before the army gets to it," Blaze told her.

Talia nodded and pulled out one of her silvery tail feathers with her beak.

"Once we pass through the portal, it will close behind us for good," she said.

Maximus nodded. The Owls of Valor, Claw, Grey, Talia, and Blaze flew into the portal.

"Wait!" Tag cried. "Bod is trapped!"

Bod had been caught by a group of rats. They held his wings down so that he couldn't fly.

Tag went to help, but Skyla pulled him back. "There's no time! The portal is closing!" she cried.

She grabbed his wing, and they fell back through the portal just as it sealed shut.

TROUBLE IN PERODIA

Tag and Skyla fell onto the bottom of a hard staircase. Tag stared at the place where the portal had been. The Underland was gone. Bod was gone.

Tag put his wing against the cold stone. "I'll come back for you," he whispered. "I promise."

There was a scuffling sound behind him.
Tag turned to see a flash of red eyes glinting
back at him.

It was Skull! And he wasn't alone. He had
ten rats with him.

"You!" Skyla yelled.

Skull grinned. "Never turn your back on
the enemy!" he laughed as he ran.

Tag and Skyla chased the rats up the
staircase. But just like the mole, the rats were
impossibly fast. As Tag turned the corner, the
rats disappeared into thin air.

When they arrived back in Grey's study, Tag fell to the ground.

"Skull!" he gasped. "He escaped!"

Tag looked up at Grey, Claw, Blaze, and Talia. "We need to go back to the Underland! We have to go back for Bod," he said.

"We're sorry, Tag," Talia said. "We had to close the portal for good. We can't let The Shadow find a way back here."

Skyla's eyes went wide. "But Bod is all alone there!" she shouted.

"It is done," Talia said. She patted Tag's shoulder.

"We will capture Skull and his small army," Grey said. "Once all is well in Perodia, we will find a way to help Bod."

Later that night, Tag and Skyla sat quietly in their tree.

"We'll find a way to get Bod back," Skyla said. "Maybe Blaze or Claw can help us."

Tag nodded slowly. "Bod saved Talia," he said. "He rescued us from the cages. We couldn't have closed the portal without him."

"He is a hero," Skyla said.

Tag looked up at the sky. Something seemed different. Then he realized what it was. "Skyla!" he said, standing up. "Look!"

Skyla gasped.

A very dark cloud swirled in the sky above. It blocked out the light of the moon and stars. Lightning flickered inside it.

"The Shadow," Tag whispered. "It has returned to Perodia after all!"

ABOUT THE AUTHOR

KATRINA CHARMAN has wanted to be a children's book writer ever since she was eleven, when her teacher asked her class to write an epilogue to Roald Dahl's *Matilda*. Katrina's teacher thought her writing was good enough to send to Roald Dahl himself! Sadly, she never got a reply, but this experience ignited her love of reading and writing. Katrina lives in England with her husband and three children. The Last Firehawk is her first early chapter book series in the U.S.

ABOUT THE ILLUSTRATOR

JUDIT TONDORA was born in Hungary and now works from her countryside studio. Her illustrations are rooted in the traditional European style but also contain elements of American mainstream style. Her characters have a vivacious retro vibe placed right into the present day: she says, "I put the good old retro together with modern style to give charisma to my illustrations."

The Underland

Questions and Activities

1. **L**ook back at the beginning of Chapter 7. Why is The Shadow still powerful even though Blaze defeated it with the Ember Stone?

2. **A** *simile* is when you use the words "like" or "as" to compare two unlike things. Can you find the simile on page 65? Write your own simile that describes Skull.

3. **R**eread page 66. What is Skull's evil plan? What does he want and why?

4. **A**t the beginning of their journey, Tag thinks that Bod is a bully. How does Tag feel about Bod by the end? Why do you think his feelings changed?

5. **G**rey gives the friends a magical lantern so they will be able to see in the Underland. If you had to travel to the Underland, what is one magical object that you would bring? Draw and label a picture of your object!